To

Makaila –
A super special young
lady, that's why
Channa wanted you
to have this book.
Blessings!
Philip Dah Smith
3-25-2000

Dear Mak,
Happy Easter
Baby. We love you
always.... Mom+Dad
2008

The Rabbit and the Promise Sign

by Pat Day-Bivins and Philip Dale Smith
illustrated by Donna Brooks

Golden Anchor Press
Tacoma, Washington

THIS BOOK IS DEDICATED--

To my father and mother, Omar Lee and Louise Rebecca Day, who taught me God's love, and to my wonderful husband, Kenneth D. Bivins, who shows me God's love. --Pat Day-Bivins

To Mary Jo Smith, my wife, who enriches each life she touches, who especially enriches mine, and who first called my attention to the rabbit in the moon. --Philip Dale Smith

To my parents, Don and Wanda Miller. To Victoria, Debbie, and Pattye--very special friends. To Donna and Jan, mentors and art colleagues. To Joe, my husband--love of my life, and especially to my sons, Bryan and Brad, who bring me great joy. --Donna Brooks

Publisher's Cataloging-in-Publication
(Provided by Quality Books, Inc)

Day-Bivins, Pat
  The rabbit and the promise sign / written by Pat Day-Bivins and Philip Dale Smith ; illustrated by Donna Brooks.
    p. cm.
    SUMMARY: Grandfather Josiah Rabbit tells the story of a rabbit who received a sign on his forehead because he stayed awake with Jesus in the Garden of Gethsemane.
    Preassigned LCCN: 97-74229
    ISBN: 1-886864-08-X

    1. Rabbits--Religious aspects--Juvenile fiction.   2. Jesus Christ--Prayer in Gethsemane--Juvenile fiction. 3. Easter--Juvenile fiction.   I. Smith, Dale, 1932- II. Brooks, Donna. III. Title.

PZ7.D39Ra 1998   [E]
                        QBI97-30326

Published by Golden Anchor Press
1801 S. 112th St., Tacoma, WA 98444
Printed in Hong Kong by C&C Offset

First Edition
9 8 7 6 5 4 3 2 1

This book is printed on acid-free paper.
(So your children can pass it on to their children)

The art for each picture is an original oil painting on canvas, which is color-separated and reproduced in full color.

Cover design by Steve Diggs & Friends, Nashville, Tennessee

Golden Anchor books are available at special discount for bulk purchases for fund-raising efforts, sales promotions or educational use. Special editions and excerpts, including prints, can be created to specification.

A MESSAGE FROM THE AUTHORS--

Did this story really happen? Clue: In real life rabbits seldom wear bow ties, and old rabbits almost never walk with canes! Is it a Bible story? No. This is a Christian fable. It's a story from the world of make-believe, but is based on the reality that we have a loving, caring Savior.

Children will enjoy this precious story. In the hands of a knowledgeable and sensitive adult, it will help them grasp the beauty and wonder of what did happen in the Garden of Gethsemane. Also, children will be better able to understand the significance of the events that followed. The closing scenes provide a lifelong visual reminder that our Lord is always near.

A subliminal message in *The Rabbit and the Promise Sign* is that God, who cares about all His creation, certainly cares about little boys and little girls.   The stars sing His praises, and the heavens declare His glory. He says, "Every animal of the forest is mine, and the cattle of a thousand hills. I know every bird in the mountains and the creatures of the field are mine." He clothes the lilies of the field. He notices every sparrow that falls. We're of greater worth than any of these. So a lonely or hurting child can know that God sees and cares about him or her, just as in this fable Jesus cares about Little Rabbit. God's love and concern come through in a way the child can understand.

Let us send you a free special report: "How to Teach God's Love Using *The Rabbit and the Promise Sign.*" It is a discussion guide with questions you can ask to help children understand the Garden of Gethsemane. It tells how to use this fable to strengthen lifelong awareness of the Creator who cares and is always near. Just send a self-addressed, stamped envelope to The Promise Sign,
PO Box 45208, Tacoma, WA 98445-0208.

Now enjoy this special story and the beautiful scenes the gifted
Donna Brooks uses to clothe the images depicted by our words.
--Pat Day-Bivins and Philip Dale Smith

P.S. If the sky is clear tonight, be sure to look
and see if you can spot the "special reminder!"

"Soon I'll be home!" thought Bo
Rabbit as he bounced happily down
the lane. "I can't wait to tell Rebecca all
about my long trip." It was a beautiful Easter
Sunday. Soft clouds floating across the bright
blue sky looked like big, fluffy snow bunnies.

Rebecca had stayed home to add bits of fur to their nursery. "Wow! Our first babies will soon be born!" Bo said. But as he neared their home under the roots of the old oak tree, he didn't see Rebecca. She usually rushed out to greet him. Where was she? Then he heard someone crying behind the tree. It was Rebecca!

"What's wrong, Rebecca?"
Bo asked gently.

"Dear Bo," she said, "We wanted to have many babies and I know you planned to be here when they were born. But I had just one baby, and he was born before you got back!"

Bo could hardly believe it. Rabbits usually have many babies at a time, but when he hurried over to the nest, he found it held just one little bunny.

Suddenly, Bo began doing rabbit flips and cartwheels. "Look at our son!" he shouted. "What a wonderful surprise! He has the Promise Sign, Rebecca. He has the Promise Sign!"

Together they looked at their baby. The bunny was already covered with soft, downy fur, and on his forehead was a *star!*

"The man's name was Jesus. He looked sad, too.

As the rabbit hopped nearer to Jesus, he sensed this special man had known and loved him for a long, long time.

"He didn't feel sad or lonely anymore. He snuggled close to the loving man.

"Jesus stroked him and said, 'Oh, Little Rabbit, you have come to be with me at this sorrowful time. I asked my friends to wait and watch, but they fell asleep. Wait now, while I talk with my Father.'"

"Little Rabbit hopped a few feet away to wait while
the man prayed. For many hours Jesus talked to the
Heavenly Father. At times He would cry, and the
little rabbit wanted to comfort Him. But he could
only stay close by. So he waited.

"Before the dawn broke, Jesus walked over to the rabbit. 'It is time for me to go, little one,' He said. 'My Father has a task that I must face alone. Thank you for waiting and watching tonight when others did not. Because of your love I will give you a special blessing. On your forehead I will place a sign that will pass to other generations of your family.

"'Each time a baby rabbit is born with the sign, the story will be told of how you stayed with me tonight. The sign will be a star, a reminder of the star that appeared over the stable in Bethlehem, where I was born.' He touched Little Rabbit on the forehead. Suddenly, a patch of white appeared--a beautiful star! Love such as he had never imagined swept over Little Rabbit.

"Jesus lovingly stroked him and arose to leave.

"As Jesus walked down the path to wake His sleeping friends, the rabbit watched Him go, then went joyfully on his way. What a wondrous night it had been!

"Little Rabbit came to the garden again the next night, and the next. Jesus was not there. Still, the rabbit felt warm and cozy as he thought about the kind, loving man."

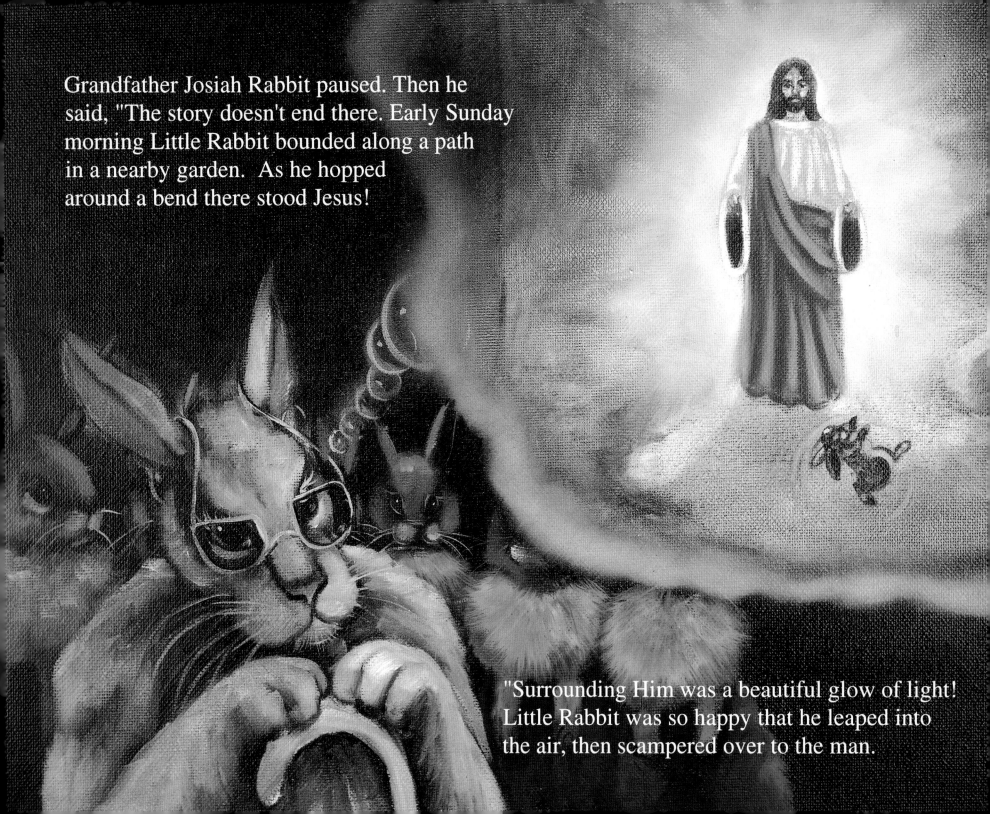

Grandfather Josiah Rabbit paused. Then he said, "The story doesn't end there. Early Sunday morning Little Rabbit bounded along a path in a nearby garden. As he hopped around a bend there stood Jesus!

"Surrounding Him was a beautiful glow of light! Little Rabbit was so happy that he leaped into the air, then scampered over to the man.

"Jesus picked him up and said, 'Little friend, I will soon go to my Father. I won't walk these paths with you again, but I promise never to be far away. When humans think of my Cross, they will know how deeply I love them. My star on your forehead will remind everyone of how you loved me and stayed close when I was alone in the garden. Your star will also be a Sign of My Promise that I will always be near you.

"'There is another reminder,' He continued. 'Tonight, look into the sky. What you see will help you remember that the Father and I love all our creatures and that we are always close by.' Placing Little Rabbit on the ground, Jesus patted him gently and went on His way.

"Little Rabbit could hardly wait to see in the sky the reminder the special man had promised. When night finally came, there it was!" Grandfather paused at this point in the story. But the excited rabbits called out, . . .

The rabbits cheered and cheered! Then each came by
to see Baby Gabriel and touch his star. As the last one
passed by, Grandfather Rabbit cried out, "Look!"

"Look, everyone, look at the beautiful star! And look
at the moon!"   All eyes turned to the heavens.

Sure enough! Near the moon was a bright star much like the star on the bunny's forehead. And on the moon was the shadowy form of a happy, dancing rabbit! On moonlit nights from now on they would see this special reminder that Jesus is always near.

As clouds moved across the sky, Grandfather said, "Sometimes we can't see the moon and the stars, but they are always there. So is our loving Heavenly Father."

Late that night Gabriel curled up by his mother and father and fell fast asleep. Bo and Rebecca looked at their son with great joy. "What a marvelous day this has been!" said Rebecca.

"The most wonderful Easter ever!" said Bo. With the moon and bright stars shining down upon them, the happy rabbits were soon sound asleep.